"THE LOST BOY"

Adapted for the stage by Millie Hardy-Sims, based on the life and works of J.M. BARRIE

Running time: 1.5 hours + Interval

Originally performed by *Happy Thoughts Drama Company* **in October 2015**

CHARACTERS
CAST SIZE: Min 14, Max 34

James Matthew Barrie .... The protagonist. Scottish. A playwright. He befriends the Llewellyn-Davies family whilst taking a stroll in the park and ends up becoming a father figure to the boys. Early 40s. Dark hair, moustache.

Mary Barrie .... Act 1 only. James' long suffering wife. Wears fancy clothing and is determined to appear higher class then she is. Can also appear as any of the actresses in the Peter Pan cast.

Sylvia Llewellyn-Davies .... Female lead. Late 30s. Mother to George, Jack, Peter, Michael and Nicholas. Widowed, potentially still in mourning. Befriends Mr. Barrie. Dies in the final scene.

Liza .... Act 1 only. The maid to the Barrie household. Can also appear as any of the actresses in the Peter Pan cast.

Porthos .... Barrie's St. Bernard dog.

Emma du Maurier .... Sylvia's sophisticated and opinionated mother. She is determined to provide the best she can for her daughter and is suspicious of Barrie and his intentions.

George Llewellyn-Davies .... 13 years old. The eldest of the boys. Tries to take care of his mother as the father figure, but still remains a child. Can be doubled as a Peter Pan actor.

John (Jack) Llewellyn-Davies .... 12 years old. The most immature of the boys. Can be doubled as a Peter Pan actor.

Peter Llewellyn-Davies .... 7 years old. The middle of the boys. After his father's death he became the man of the house and grew up too quickly. He is the inspiration for the character of Peter Pan.

Michael Llewellyn-Davies .... 4 years old. The second youngest of the boys. He is very immature and initiates most of the pretend games.

Nicholas Llewellyn-Davies .... 1 year old. Portrayed by a baby doll.

Charles Frohman .... Late 40s. American. Barrie's theatre producer. Sarcastic personality.

Gerald du Maurier/Captain Hook .... Early 30s. Sylvia's brother, an actor. He becomes a close friend of James' and portrays Captain Hook in the production.

Gilbert Canaan .... 40s. Mary Barrie's lover.

Actors in 'Peter Pan'
    Nina Boucicault (Peter Pan)
    Hilda Trevelyan (Wendy Darling)
    George Horsee (John Darling)
    Winifred Geogeghan (Michael Darling)
    Arthur Lupino (Nana)
    Mermaids x2
    Fairies x2
    Pirates
    Indians

ORIGINAL CAST
October 2015 Production

J.M. Barrie	Rowan M.
Sylvia Llewelyn-Davies	Kelly P.
Mary Barrie/Nina Boucicault	Amy C.
Liza/Hilda Trevelyan	Megan S.
Emma DuMaurier	Georgia D-B.
Gerald DuMaurier	Lewis H.
Charles Frohman/Porthos	Harry D-B.
George Llewelyn-Davies	Leo M.
Jack Llewelyn-Davies	Morgan G.
Peter Llewelyn-Davies	Heather P.
Michael Llewelyn-Davies	Emily-Rose L.
Gilbert Canaan	Christian H.

ADVICE FOR STAGING

The only consistent piece of staging is a bench downstage right, and a large window upstage right that can open.

The Lost Boy | 3

LIST OF PROPS

These props are suggested from the original performance.

Nicholas doll

Park bench

Picnic blanket

Kite

Newspaper

Edwardian pram

Pirate steering wheel

Native American drums

Edwardian style sofa (and chair)

Coffee table

End table

Tea tray

Reading book

Large dining table

9x chairs

Dining equipment (cutlery, glasses, food and crockery)

Double window/doors

3x beds

SCENES

SCENE 1: THE PARK	6
SCENE 2: DUKE OF YORK'S THEATRE	8
SCENE 3: BARRIE MANOR	9
SCENE 4: PARK	11
SCENE 5: BARRIE MANOR	17
SCENE 6: PARK	20
SCENE 7: BARRIE MANOR	27
SCENE 8: BARRIE MANOR – DINING ROOM	29
SCENE 9: PARK	37
SCENE 10: THEATRE	43
SCENE 11: BARRIE MANOR	45
SCENE 13: THEATRE	52
SCENE 14: PARK	58
SCENE 15: THEATRE - OPENING NIGHT	60

SCENE 1: THE PARK

CURTAINS, or a DARK FLY, REMAIN CLOSED.

A bench stands DOWNSTAGE RIGHT.

BARRIE and PORTHOS enter STAGE LEFT. BARRIE wears a bowler hat and carries his newspaper under his arm. The other arm holds PORTHOS' lead and a cane. BARRIE walks over to the bench and sits on it, placing PORTHOS' lead beside him along with the cane.

BARRIE: Well now Porthos, shall we see what the damage is this time?

PORTHOS barks.

BARRIE opens the newspaper and flicks through to the 'review page'.

BARRIE: Ah, here we are – 'Little Mary' by J. M. Barrie. "Little Mary- produced in London last evening... the Times says the play is a..." Oh dear. Oh this is not good. Not good at all. Listen here, "A mere trifle, an impudent little trifle. We make haste to laugh lest we weep entirely." This is not good at all my lad. Charles will not be happy.

BARRIE shuts the newspaper and folds it onto his lap. He sighs heavily.

EMMA and GERALD enter REAR OF AUDITORIUM, strolling casually. EMMA hangs off GERALD'S arm.

They reach the front of the audience – within range of BARRIE.

EMMA: Did you hear about that play last night, the new one from that Barrie fellow?

GERALD: Apparently it flopped entirely. Poor man.

BARRIE inclines his head, listening.

EMMA: I think the fellow should focus more on his marriage than pursuing such a trifle of a career. I heard from Mrs. Beecham that his wife is considering leaving him.

BARRIE gets to his feet and picks up his cane and PORTHOS' lead. He walks past EMMA and tips his hat.

BARRIE: Mrs. duMaurier.

BARRIE exits STAGE LEFT with PORTHOS.

EMMA: Wasn't that...?

GERALD: Mother, can you not keep your gossiping tongue silenced?

EMMA: (defensively) I said nothing he won't already know. Come on dear, Sylvia and the boys are coming around for tea tonight.

ALL EXIT REAR OF AUDITORIUM.

CURTAINS UP.

SCENE 2: DUKE OF YORK'S THEATRE

2x STAGEHANDS enter, carrying props from one side to the other (as though dismantling a show). A SOFA and END TABLE are set CENTRE STAGE.

CHARLES FROHMAN stands centre stage with his arms folded. BARRIE enters STAGE LEFT, straight from the park.

BARRIE: (Removing hat) Good afternoon Charles.

CHARLES: Care to explain?

BARRIE: About the play? I am very sorry.

CHARLES: We've cancelled the show. Can't risk losing money.

BARRIE: I understand it wasn't the best, but cancelled?

CHARLES: Yes, cancelled. Most of the audience demanded their money back; they were so appalled! We can't afford it, James. I can't afford it.

BARRIE: Just give me one more chance, Charles. One more play, one more opening night? I promise it will be worth it. Have a little faith.

CHARLES: That's what you promised last time, James.

BARRIE: Please.

PAUSE. CHARLES sighs heavily.

CHARLES: One more chance.

BARRIE: It will be amazing, just you wait.

CHARLES: I am trusting you.

BARRIE: You won't regret it!

BARRIE leaves the way he came. CHARLES shakes his head.

CHARLES: Yes, James. I have complete faith... that I am a fool.

CHARLES exits STAGE RIGHT.

SCENE 3: BARRIE MANOR

LIZA enters carrying a tea tray. She sets it on the end table. She then proceeds to dust around.

MARY enters STAGE LEFT.

MARY: (To JAMES, offstage) And do you have an idea for this new play?

MARY sits on the sofa. BARRIE enters STAGE LEFT. He has removed his hat and coat – it is later in the day.

BARRIE: Not yet, but I am sure one will come.

MARY: Charles seemed awfully final about it.

BARRIE: Charles is an awfully final sort of person.

BARRIE picks up the teapot.

BARRIE: Tea, dear?

BARRIE pours the tea.

MARY: I don't know what to tell you James. I'm not sure you can pull it off this time.

BARRIE hands MARY her teacup and sits beside her with his.

BARRIE: Something will come to me.

MARY: When, James? When it's too late? We can't afford for you to be a failure.

BARRIE: You think me a failure?

MARY: Would you like to read the newspaper review again?

BARRIE lowers his head and sips his tea.

MARY: I just thank God we have no children to support. I'm not sure you would manage it.

BARRIE: Thank you, Mary. That's enough.

MARY looks at him, blankly. There is a pause while BARRIE avoids her gaze. MARY stands, puts her tea on the tray and leaves STAGE LEFT.

BARRIE stares blankly ahead. LIZA continues dusting behind him.

BARRIE: What do you think, Liza?

LIZA: I'm not sure it's my place to say, Sir.

BARRIE: Och, Mary's right. I am a failure. Maybe it is just as well we have no children.

LIZA: You mustn't think that way, Sir. If you don't mind my saying, I'm sure you'd make a wonderful father.

BARRIE: If only I'd make a wonderful writer.

BARRIE sits back in his chair and sips his tea.

LIZA: Inspiration will come, Sir. When you least expect it.

LIZA begins clearing up the tea things.

LIZA: Are you finished, Sir?

BARRIE doesn't respond, still staring ahead.

LIZA: Mr. Barrie?

BARRIE: Hmm? Oh, yes.

LIZA takes the cup off him.

LIZA: You were away with the fairies there, Sir.

BARRIE: Fairies?

LIZA exits STAGE LEFT with the tea tray.

BARRIE shuts his eyes. 2x FAIRIES enter STAGE RIGHT and pirouette DOWNSTAGE. As they dance, the CURTAIN lowers.

SCENE 4: PARK

The fairies continue to dance until BARRIE enters with PORTHOS. He carries a notepad. He sits on the bench and begins to write. PORTHOS stands beside the bench, though gradually begins to fall asleep. BARRIE continues to write – crossing out sometimes.

SYLVIA enters REAR AUDITORIUM with all 5 boys.

MICHAEL: Yay! A day without grandmother! Freedom!

SYLVIA: Michael!

GEORGE stands in front of the audience, hands on hips.

GEORGE: I am King George the Eighteenth, you must kneel before me!

JACK kneels, and pulls MICHAEL down beside him.

MICHAEL: Ow, Jack!

JACK: He said kneel!

GEORGE: Lowly villagers, I have rescued you from the terrible beastie!

JACK: Oh, King George! We thank you humbly!

MICHAEL: Can I get up now? My knees hurt.

GEORGE: Scurvy knave, thou shalt not complain in front of the king! En garde!

SYLVIA laughs and ascends the steps to DOWNSTAGE LEFT. GEORGE, MICHAEL and JACK duel each other.

SYLVIA: Here, Peter, lay out the blanket. (She coughs) Good boy.

PETER takes the blanket and lays it on the ground.

PETER: Here, Mother.

PETER takes NICHOLAS from SYLVIA and sits on the floor with him.

SYLVIA: Thank you darling.

SYLVIA sits beside him on the blanket. They watch the boys play.

SYLVIA: Don't you want to play?

PETER: Playing is for children.

SYLVIA shakes her head sadly at PETER.

GEORGE defeats MICHAEL.

GEORGE: Fool, you shall be thrown in the dungeon.

MICHAEL: On what charges?!

GEORGE: Being foul, odious and my little brother! Take him away!

JACK: Yes Sire!

JACK takes MICHAEL'S arm and leads him up the RIGHT steps. He pushes him under the bench.
BARRIE doesn't notice. MICHAEL lies under the bench.

JACK: If you try to escape, you'll wake the slumbering beast.

JACK returns to GEORGE.

JACK: Sire, he is imprisoned in the eternal chamber.

GEORGE: Excellent work! Now, we ride for fair maiden!

GEORGE and JACK 'ride' up to the blanket.

BARRIE grunts and pulls a page from his notebook, scrumpling it up. He does so with such ferocity he drops his notebook. He bends to pick it up and notices MICHAEL beneath his bench.

BARRIE: Hello there, you appear to be beneath my bench?

MICHAEL: I have no choice, Sir. Orders are orders.

BARRIE: Under whose orders might I ask?

The Lost Boy | 12

MICHAEL: King George. He is the most ferocious and tyrannical ruler the world has ever known.

BARRIE: You must have done something awful to cross such an evil king. What are your charges?

MICHAEL: Being foul, obi..oli...odi-ous... and his little brother.

BARRIE: I see, there is no greater crime than that I am afraid.

MICHAEL: Commander Jack says if I try to escape then the slumbering beast will gobble me all up.

BARRIE: Slumbering beast?

MICHAEL points at PORTHOS.

BARRIE: Och, this is indeed the worst beast ever imagined. It is the great crocodile, whose soul goal is to gobble up everything in its path. See his teeth – sharper than knives.

MICHAEL: How ghastly!

BARRIE: It is said he once swallowed an alarm clock, and now an ominous ticking comes from the depth of his belly. Listen...

BARRIE pulls out his pocket watch and holds it so MICHAEL can hear.

BARRIE: Do you hear?

MICHAEL: (gasps) I do indeed hear it Sir!

BARRIE: I would stay safe in the dungeon if I were you.

GEORGE hurries over.

GEORGE: Excuse me Sir, is my brother bothering you?

BARRIE: You must be Commander Jack? Or could it be you are the ferocious and tyrannical King George?

GEORGE: The latter, Sir.

BARRIE stands and bows deeply.

BARRIE: I pray I do not offend such an iron fisted ruler.

GEORGE and MICHAEL giggle. JACK hurries over.

JACK: George, Mother tells us to stop pestering this gentleman.

PORTHOS wakes up and barks.

BARRIE: The beast! He has awoken!

PORTHOS begins to sniff MICHAEL.

MICHAEL: No! Don't eat me! I'm too young to die!

BARRIE: I shall rescue you, Sire!

BARRIE 'tackles' PORTHOS, ending up on his back on the floor. PORTHOS spins and begins licking BARRIE.

BARRIE: Now he's got me! Help!

MICHAEL crawls out from under the bench and jumps on PORTHOS.

MICHAEL: I will save you Sir!

PORTHOS begins licking MICHAEL, who descends in a fit of laughter. SYLVIA hurries over.

SYLVIA: I do apologise for my boys, Sir!

BARRIE gets to his feet.

BARRIE: No need, there is no harm in it.

BARRIE dusts himself off.

BARRIE: I am James Barrie.

BARRIE holds out his hand for SYLVIA to shake.

SYLVIA: The writer? How lovely to meet you. Sylvia Llewellyn-Davies. You've already met my boys. George, Jack, Michael... and Peter and Nicholas are over there.

BARRIE: It is lovely to meet you all.

GEORGE: What is your dog called, Mr. Barrie?

MICHAEL: It's not a dog, it's a giant crocodile that swallowed an alarm clock.

SYLVIA: Michael...

MICHAEL: It is! Tell them!

BARRIE: I am afraid I was imagining with Michael.

SYLVIA: Well, he seems to be enjoying it.

BARRIE smiles.

BARRIE: His name is Porthos, George.

GEORGE: Like the Musketeer? All for one and one for all!

GEORGE begins 'duelling' with JACK again. MICHAEL follows them along with PORTHOS.

SYLVIA: I do apologise again, my boys can be a little full on.

BARRIE: It's the joy of youth, Mrs. Llewellyn-Davies.

SYLVIA: They seem to have enjoyed meeting you. It's so lovely to see them all so happy.

BARRIE: We're here every day and Porthos is always happy to play games.

SYLVIA: Then I'm sure we will meet again, Sir.

BARRIE: I look forward to it.

BARRIE bows his head. SYLVIA curtseys minutely and walks back to the blanket. The BOYS all run over.

BARRIE: Porthos! (whistles) Here boy!

PORTHOS hurries over to BARRIE. BARRIE strokes PORTHOS' ears.

BARRIE: Ticking crocodile? I wonder...

LLEWELLYN-DAVIES exit.

SCENE 5: BARRIE MANOR

Curtains rise, revealing BARRIE LIVING ROOM.

MARY sits on the sofa, reading a letter and holding a book.

BARRIE enters, removing his hat from the park.
MARY hides the letter within the book.

MARY: I was beginning to wonder whether you were in fact coming home. It is getting late.

BARRIE: Sorry Mary, I didn't notice.

BARRIE sits on the sofa and begins writing in his notebook.

MARY: (sniffily) Did you get much written?

BARRIE doesn't respond.

MARY: James?

BARRIE: (jerking to) Yes, lovely day.

MARY: That is not what I asked.

BARRIE: Sorry dear, I just had to write that down.

MARY: And what is that?

BARRIE: I met a wee lad in the park today. He imagined that Porthos was a great ticking crocodile! Can you imagine?

MARY: Did he now?

BARRIE: His Mother was there, a lovely woman.

MARY: (**sniffily**) Has she a name?

BARRIE: Mrs. Llewellyn-Davies.

MARY: The widow?

BARRIE: I never asked. I didn't think it proper.

MARY: Everyone knows the story. She is the daughter of George duMaurier, the writer, and his wife. She married Arthur Llewellyn-Davies, a barrister by trade, who promptly fell ill and died, leaving her with five children and no income to speak of.

BARRIE: How awful. I had no idea.

MARY: If you socialised at your performances you may learn a thing or two. We met her and her husband at the Clarke's dinner party several years ago.

BARRIE: I thought I recognised her. How awful to be without a husband.

MARY: I sometimes know the feeling.

BARRIE: Sorry?

MARY: We should have them round for a dinner party. Mrs. Llewellyn-Davies and her mother.

BARRIE: And the boys?

MARY: If we must.

BARRIE: They really are fantastic. Such imaginations. I felt like a wee lad again.

MARY: Gilbert called round again today. Are you in trouble, James?

BARRIE: No, not trouble. I should imagine he wished to see me about the finances.

MARY: Are we in trouble?

BARRIE: No my dear. Nothing that Gilbert cannot fix.

MARY: Well, he said he would stop round again sometime this week. Will you be here?

BARRIE: How can one possibly know if one is not given a specific time.

BARRIE begins to write again.

MARY: Gilbert is a very accomplished gentleman. He was telling me about his degree.

BARRIE: Really?

MARY: You don't have a degree, James.

BARRIE: No dear.

MARY begins to read the letter again, hoping to provoke a response. LIZA enters and stands.

LIZA: Excuse me Ma'am, Master, dinner is ready.

MARY gets to her feet. LIZA exits.

MARY: Unfortunately all children must grow up eventually. Will you be joining me for dinner tonight?

BARRIE: Aye. I'll be right there.

MARY exits. BARRIE stares straight ahead.

BARRIE: All children must grow up?

**BARRIE scribbles hastily in his notebook.
LIGHTS fade.**

SCENE 6: PARK

GEORGE, JACK and MICHAEL run down the side of the audience, banging their hands over their mouths in a Native American style. THE BOYS run up onto the stage. GEORGE stops in the middle and holds up his hand for the others to stop.

GEORGE: Halt! I am big chief flying goose and I order big party to bring up the sun.

JACK: (laughing) Flying goose! Silly goose more like!

JACK and MICHAEL fall about the floor laughing.

GEORGE: Silence! You, (**points at JACK**) fluffy duck, scout territory, look out for white-skins.

JACK stands on the edge and looks out over the audience, scouting.

GEORGE: Bear cub, you light fire. I start dance.

MICHAEL begins 'lighting a fire'. GEORGE starts to dance around in a circle, beating his hand over his mouth.

From behind the curtain comes another Native call. BARRIE enters through the curtain, beating his hand over his mouth. He stops in front of GEORGE and holds his arms crossed and firm. PORTHOS bounds in and lies beside SYLVIA, a kite in his mouth.

BARRIE: How! I heard this is the camp of Big Chief Flying Goose, feared leader of this tribe of Pickaninnys.

GEORGE: I am Big Chief Flying Goose, this is my tribe! Who told you of us?!

BARRIE: Pale face squaw with cub, standing by wild river.

GEORGE: Who are you!

BARRIE: (**bowing on knees, head on the floor**) I am Inky-finger, writer of many great stories and singer of many songs. I ask humbly to join your fearsome tribe.

JACK: He look like cowboy man to me, Chief. Me think no good.

GEORGE: Are you a boy of cows, Inky-finger?

BARRIE: **(getting to his feet)** I am not boy of cows great Chief.

GEORGE: Tell me, Inky-finger, what makes the red man red?

BARRIE: Earth, Chief.

GEORGE: He is outsider, tie him up and roast him on fire!

JACK and MICHAEL cheer and grab BARRIE's arms.

GEORGE: Red man red because he blush. Silly man not know that.

BARRIE: A mistake Chief, a mistake!

GEORGE: Roast him!

BARRIE manages to escape and begins to run towards the back of the audience. He ducks into an aisle to hide. JACK, GEORGE and MICHAEL run after him and straight past, around the whole audience. BARRIE hurries out of his hiding place and back up to SYLVIA, who is laughing.

SYLVIA: I see the boys have got you on the run, Mr. Barrie.

BARRIE: So it would seem!

SYLVIA: What is it this time?

BARRIE: They think I am a cowboy, trying to integrate their Indian tribe.

SYLVIA: Such a magical imagination you have, Sir, such that I do not possess, want of practice.

BARRIE: My mother used to say 'want of practice means you have stopped believing'.

SYLVIA: She seems a wise woman.

BARRIE: Aye, she was.

BARRIE clears his throat. He nods at PETER, who is sat reading behind SYLVIA.

BARRIE: A good book?

SYLVIA: Yes, Alice in Wonderland – have you read it?

BARRIE: One of my favourites.

SYLVIA: Peter loves reading. Sometimes he reads a little too much and loses track of time.

BARRIE: That is the best place to be I find.

SYLVIA: I struggled to convince the other boys to pick up a book, let alone read it. Too much work, they said.

BARRIE: Nothing is really work unless you'd rather be doing something else.

SYLVIA: You say such marvellous things Mr. Barrie.

BARRIE smiles, then adjusts his collar awkwardly.

BARRIE: Mary, my wife, asked if you and the boys would like to join us at our home on Saturday afternoon for a garden party?

SYLVIA: How kind!

BARRIE: Your Mother is welcome too, of course. Mary is dying to meet Mrs. duMaurier.

SYLVIA: I'm sure she would love to come, and Gerald too, my brother, if that is alright.

BARRIE: Aye.

SYLVIA: Thank you Mr. Barrie.

BARRIE: It is our pleasure.

GEORGE, JACK and MICHAEL run back up the aisle, pointing at BARRIE.

GEORGE: There he is!

JACK: Let's capture that man!

BARRIE: (**to Sylvia**) Excuse me.

MICHAEL and JACK pounce on BARRIE, dragging him to the ground.

GEORGE: Any last words, boy of cows?

BARRIE: To die would be an awfully big adventure.

PORTHOS barks from SYLVIA'S side and jumps on top of the pile.

JACK: The Indian has a wolf! Run!

GEORGE, JACK and MICHAEL stumble away. MICHAEL falls onto PETER.

PETER: Ouch! Watch where you are going Michael, you buffoon.

MICHAEL: Sorry Peter.

GEORGE: I say Peter, he was only playing a game.

PETER: Well he shouldn't.

BARRIE: With all due respect, lad, Michael is only a wee boy. What do you think a wee boy should be doing?

PETER: Learning to read and write and make a name for himself.

SYLVIA: Peter...

BARRIE: Are you not a wee lad yourself, Peter?

PETER: One of us had to grow up.

SYLVIA: Peter! That's quite enough.

BARRIE: It's alright, the lad has a point.

PETER: I do?

BARRIE: You may have needed to grow up, but that doesn't mean you should let go of being young.

PETER: Says the grown man painted like a red Indian.

BARRIE: Because I held onto my inner boy. Here, I'll prove it. Who would like to fly a kite?

MICHAEL: Yes please!

BARRIE crosses to the blanket and picks up PORTHOS' discarded kite.

BARRIE: This was mine when I was wee. I thought I would bring it today. Here, Michael, take this.

BARRIE hands the frame to MICHAEL.

BARRIE: Hold on tight lad. Peter, would you like the string?

PETER: No.

SYLVIA: Peter... don't spoil it.

PETER: I don't want to fly a kite.

BARRIE: It's alright, perhaps next time. Jack, how about you? George you can have the next turn.

JACK eagerly takes the string from BARRIE.

BARRIE: When I give the word, Michael, I need you to run like the wind is biting your heels. Do you think you can do that?

MICHAEL: I am willing to try, Sir.

BARRIE: Good lad. Jack, hold on tight to that line.

SYLVIA: Wait! (**she pulls the ribbon from her hair**) A kite should have a tail.

BARRIE: Good thinking Madam.

SYLVIA ties her ribbon to the kite frame.

SYLVIA: There, the best there ever was.

BARRIE: (bending down) Are you ready Michael?

MICHAEL nods.

BARRIE: Then run lad!

MICHAEL begins to run.

BARRIE: Release it!

MICHAEL lets go of the frame. The kite is lifted into the air for a moment, then drops to the ground.

MICHAEL picks it up sadly.

MICHAEL: Did I do it wrong?

BARRIE: Not at all, but you see – we hadn't enough faith. In order to fly, one must believe wholly and completely. Faith and trust is all it takes. Let's all shut our eyes a moment.

SYLVIA and the BOYS (minus PETER) close their eyes.

BARRIE: Imagine the wind wrapping its tender arms around the kite and pulling it up into the heavens. Imagine it and believe with all your being. Are you doing so?

GEORGE: Yes!

BARRIE: Right, Michael, try again. Believe. Faith and trust.

GEORGE, JACK, SYLVIA: Faith and trust Michael!

MICHAEL starts to run again.

GEORGE, JACK and SYLVIA: Faith and trust! Faith and trust! (**continue chanting**)

PETER shuts his eyes.

PETER: (whispered) Faith and trust.

BARRIE: Let go Michael!

MICHAEL lets go. The kite lifts into the air.

MICHAEL: It's working!

BARRIE: Because we all believed! Look at it soar!

SYLVIA: It's beautiful!

GEORGE: Well done Michael!

BARRIE notices PETER with his eyes closed, mouthing 'faith and trust'. He smiles thoughtfully.

BARRIE: Why don't you take the kite off down by the river?

JACK: Truly, Mr. Barrie!

BARRIE: Truly. Be careful of pirates now.

MICHAEL: We will, Sir!

GEORGE: Come on Peter!

**GEORGE, JACK, MICHAEL and PETER exit.
SYLVIA bundles up the blanket, then steps next to BARRIE.**

SYLVIA: Thank you Mr. Barrie, for restoring my sons faith.

BARRIE: He never lost it, only his ability to believe.

SYLVIA: Believe in what exactly?

BARRIE: Magic.

**LIGHTS FADE.
ACTORS exit.**

SCENE 7: BARRIE MANOR

CURTAINS OPEN.
LIGHTS RISE.

MARY sits on the sofa, GILBERT CANAAN beside her. They are laughing.

MARY: Oh, Mr. Canaan, you are funny!

GILBERT: You are too kind, Mrs. Barrie.

LIZA enters with a tea tray.

LIZA: Tea, Ma'am?

MARY: Oh yes, Liza. I thought you'd gotten lost!

LIZA: No, Ma'am. Apologies.

MARY: Never mind. Mr. Canaan, how would you like your tea?

GILBERT: Just a little milk, thank you.

LIZA pours tea.

LIZA: Apologies, Ma'am, but will Mr. Barrie not be joining you?

MARY: My husband is currently on his daily outing to the park. He has friends there, you see. I doubt he will be joining us anytime soon.

LIZA looks between them suspiciously.

LIZA: Will that be all Ma'am?

MARY: Yes, thank you Liza.

LIZA curtseys and exits. MARY takes a teacup and passes it to GILBERT, then takes her own.

GILBERT: I was thinking, Mrs. Barrie. If we are to work closely together, perhaps you had better start calling me Gilbert.

MARY: Only if you don't think it too impertinent.

GILBERT: Not at all. I believe we are friends now, are we not?

MARY: Then I suppose you had best call me Mary.

A flirtatious look passes between them.

GILBERT: Might I add... Mary... and do tell me if you think me too bold, but I am enjoying your company...

without Mr. Barrie. You have quite a personality.

MARY: I was once an actress you know?

GILBERT: Oh, I know. I saw you once at the Playhouse. How good of you to give it up for your husband.

MARY: He is a simple soul, my husband. Quite the lost boy. I felt he needed looking after.

GILBERT: You are the perfect model of a wife, Mary. Your husband doesn't know what he is missing.

**LIGHTS FADE.
GILBERT and MARY exit.**

SCENE 8: BARRIE MANOR – DINING ROOM

CURTAINS OPEN.
LIGIITS RISE.

A table sits to the RIGHT of the stage. LIZA sets the table for dinner. PORTHOS enters and begins to bound around LIZA'S legs. LIZA giggles.

LIZA: Oh, Porthos, really! Calm down, you big brute.

PORTHOS jumps up at LIZA, who laughs and strokes behind his ears.

LIZA: You are a daft thing, aren't you? As lovely as you are, my dear, you can't be in here when the mistress comes in. You know she won't like you being around the dinner things.

PORTHOS barks.

LIZA: Now, don't give me that. You know Mr. Barrie allows you to run riot most of the time. You must behave for him today. If only for the Mistress's benefit. You know how important she regards Madam DuMaurier.

MARY enters in her evening dress. LIZA snaps to attention and continues setting the table. PORTHOS exits swiftly.

MARY: Can you believe it Liza? He's invited them here. Everything must be perfect, do you hear?

LIZA: Yes Ma'am.

MARY: I won't have one knife out of place, not with Madam duMaurier coming.

LIZA: Yes Ma'am.

MARY: Perhaps I should have hired a butler for the occasion.

LIZA: I'm sure I'm perfectly capable, Ma'am.

MARY: Well. We shall see, won't we?

LIZA: I suppose so, Ma'am.

BARRIE: (**offstage**) Just through there, Madam duMaurier. My wife will be there to greet you.

EMMA: (**offstage**) Very good, Mr. Barrie.

EMMA DUMAURIER enters, followed by JACK, GEORGE, MICHAEL and PETER. LIZA curtseys and exits.

MARY: Madam duMaurier! (**she curtseys**) Welcome to my home. I trust my husband was welcoming?

EMMA: Ever so. What a quaint house you have.

MARY: Thank you Ma'am. I try to keep it well.

EMMA: You can but try can't you?

PORTHOS comes bounding in.

BOYS: Porthos!

MARY: Porthos! Down boy!

GEORGE: It's alright, Mrs. Barrie. We don't mind.

EMMA: George. Manners.

GEORGE: Sorry Grandmama.

LIZA enters.

LIZA: Dinner is almost served, Ma'am, if you wish to take your seats.

MARY: Thank you Liza. Madam duMaurier (**she gestures to a seat**) If you would, Madam. I'm sure my husband will be along shortly.

EMMA: Thank you. (**she sits**) Mr. Barrie is showing my son and daughter the furnishings in the day room, I believe.

MARY: (**sitting**) Oh yes. He is proud of them. They were his mothers.

EMMA: How ... humble. Boys.

The Lost Boy | 30

JACK: Where does Porthos sit, Mrs. Barrie?

MARY: In the garden, where dogs belong.

EMMA: Quite right.

MICHAEL: He'll get frightened all alone outside.

EMMA: Michael!

MICHAEL: Sorry Grandmama.

The BOYS sit with hanged heads.

SYLVIA, GERALD and BARRIE enter.

BARRIE: (mid conversation) ...all the way from Kirrimuir, if you believe.

SYLVIA: How delightful.

BARRIE: Sorry we're late dear. I was just showing Sylvia and Gerald...

MARY: The furnishings, I know. Please. Sit.

BARRIE and GERALD share a look of henpecked understanding as they sit. SYLVIA sits too, stroking PORTHOS on the way past.

LIZA enters with a tray.

BARRIE: Can you manage, Liza?

LIZA: I think so Sir, thank you.

MARY: Such wonderful grandchildren you have, Madam duMaurier.

EMMA: I try my hardest with them, though they do like to test me so.

She chucks GEORGE under the chin, who winces.

EMMA: Have you no children of your own, Mrs. Barrie?

MARY: James and I have not been so lucky.

BARRIE awkwardly clears his throat and catches GERALD'S eye. GERALD splutters as he tries not to laugh.

GERALD: What if my children do not behave, Mama. (**to the BARRIE'S**) My wife is expecting, you see.

BARRIE: How grand!

EMMA: With any luck your children will be girls. Any well-to-do person knows that one girl is worth more than twenty boys.

EMMA laughs at her own joke. MARY laughs cooperatively.

GERALD: Well, there we have it.

MARY: James told me you had five children, Ms. Llewelyn-Davies? What a handful that must be!

SYLVIA: Oh yes, that is true. But I wouldn't have it any other way. My youngest, Nicholas, is kindly in the care of Gerald's wife Muriel tonight. We thought it might be good practice for her.

MARY: How kind. You should have brought your wife, Mr. duMaurier.

GERALD: She will be happy to think you asked after her, Mrs. Barrie. Perhaps when she has recovered from birth.

MARY: (**Addressing the children**) And don't you all look lovely in your best suits.

EMMA: Persuading them to wear them was somewhat a struggle.

GERALD swigs a drink with a thankful nod towards LIZA.

GERALD: The boys are rather opinionated, Mr. Barrie, as I'm sure you've noticed.

BARRIE: I wouldn't say opinionated is such a bad thing.

GERALD: Quite right too. They are only children after all.

BARRIE smiles, finding a kindred spirit in GERALD.

GERALD: (**turning to MARY**) A lovely home you have, Mrs. Barrie.

MARY: I believe a woman should take as much pride in her home as with her appearance.

EMMA: Well said Mrs. Barrie. If only my daughter felt that way.

SYLVIA: Mother.

GERALD rolls his eyes at BARRIE who chuckles.

EMMA: Day after day I prompt her to at least hire a housekeeper to keep on top of the housework. She insists on doing it all herself. How positively medieval!

SYLVIA: I have the help of Lily, Mother.

EMMA: Lily is a maid, not a housekeeper.

SYLVIA: Mother, not now.

EMMA: (**to Mary**) Since her husband died Sylvia has somewhat struggled around the house. I offer to help when I can but she can be rather stubborn.

GERALD: (**quietly to JACK and MICHAEL**) I wonder where she gets that from.

The boys giggle. BARRIE drinks so as not to chuckle.

EMMA: Gerald, I thank you not to speak in that manner.

GERALD: Oh Mother, we are guests at a dinner party. There is no need to keep showing off about your wealth and talking your daughter down in front of her children and friends.

EMMA falls silent. The boys and SYLVIA giggle again. GERALD drinks triumphantly. They all eat in silence for a pause.

GERALD: Now, James, the boys tell me you are writing a play. Might I ask the subject?

GEORGE: Oh yes, Mr. Barrie, do tell Uncle Gerry!

BARRIE: The subject thus far is magic.

The Lost Boy | 33

GERALD: How thrilling! I've always been a believer myself.

JACK: Tell Uncle Gerry about the Indians!

GERALD: Indians?

BARRIE: There is a tribe of Indians in the play, though their part is yet to pan out.

GERALD: And the main character?

BARRIE: To be decided. The spirit of youth, I gather.

MARY scoffs.

GERALD: Spectacular!

MICHAEL: There are fairies too!

BARRIE: Yes, there are fairies too.

GERALD: It seems to me a fascinating synopsis, if patchy. It seems something Arthur would have enjoyed.

The conversation dies out. They all eat in silence.

BARRIE: I say, Madam duMaurier, how would you like a stroll around the grounds between courses? An unorthodox approach perhaps but I pride myself on that. It is not quite dark yet, and the duck pond looks lovely this time of year, and Mary can show you her prize apple tree.

MARY shoots BARRIE a warning look.

EMMA: You grow apples, Mrs. Barrie?

MARY: Since I was a girl.

EMMA: Sylvia. Will you accompany your mother?

SYLVIA: Of course.

MARY stands and SYLVIA and EMMA do too.

BARRIE: Boys, you may get down. Liza will take you to find some bread to feed the ducks if you would like?

**LIZA curtseys. The boys stand or get down. JACK, GEORGE and MICHAEL exit STAGE LEFT with LIZA.
PETER stops at SYLVIA.**

PETER: Must I, Mother?

SYLVIA: Be polite, Peter.

PETER follows his brothers. MARY leads the way OFFSTAGE RIGHT, followed by EMMA and SYLVIA.

BARRIE goes to follow but GERALD clears his throat.

GERALD: We'll be along in a moment, I need to talk to Mr. Barrie.

BARRIE steps back again. GERALD pulls out a pipe.

GERALD: Do you mind?

BARRIE: Go ahead.

GERALD: Mama hates me smoking in front of the children.

GERALD lights his pipe and puffs it a few times before talking.

GERALD: He was a good man, Arthur. He cared very much for my sister.

BARRIE: I have heard great things about him. I am sorry for the tragic loss.

GERALD: It sent a rift through the family, especially with young Peter. He looked to his father so. It tore him apart to lose him. He grew up too quickly.

BARRIE: I understand. I lost my older brother when I was wee. It broke my mother so badly I felt I had to fill his space.

GERALD: So you understand? Peter needs to learn what it is to be a child again. He doesn't listen to me. But you...

BARRIE: I don't want to impose.

The Lost Boy | 35

GERALD: Not even with my blessing? Arthur was a wonderful father, who doted on his sons. He would take them out at night to gaze at the stars. Stars are beautiful, but they must not play a part in anything. They must just look on forever. Arthur found fascination with far off lands of wonder, something magical of them, he would say, just like in your play.

BARRIE: My play?

GERALD: Magic, James. I recall as Arthur lay dying he told the boys that he would be waiting for them on one of those stars. Second to the right, he said, and straight on until morning.

BARRIE: Second to the right and straight on until morning? What a funny address that would be.

GERALD: Peter needs to find the magic again, James. You have my blessing to support my sister and her family, if not for her then for Peter. He needs to find faith, for to have faith is to have wings.

GERALD exits STAGE RIGHT. BARRIE frowns to himself, then pulls out his notebook and scribbles in it.

LIGHTS FADE.

SCENE 9: PARK

LIGHTS RISE.

IN FRONT OF CURTAINS.

EMMA and SYLVIA enter, strolling. SYLVIA carries NICHOLAS. PETER sits on the bench, swinging his legs.

EMMA: I don't like him, Sylvia. I tell you.

SYLVIA: That's nothing new for you, Mother. You don't like most.

EMMA: I'll thank you for not taking that tone with me.

SYLVIA: Oh Mother. You know you felt that way about Arthur.

EMMA: Yes, well. Arthur proved himself.

SYLVIA: As will Mr. Barrie, you just need to give him a chance.

EMMA: Then there is the problem of his wife.

SYLVIA: Mother, I don't know what you are thinking of Mr. Barrie and I but I assure you we are simply friends, and that is how it will stay. Mr. Barrie loves his wife dearly.

EMMA: Are you sure of that?

SYLVIA: Mother, I am tired of this conversation. You must learn to keep your opinions to yourself.

EMMA: What are you going to do about Peter?

SYLVIA: What about Peter?

EMMA: He is troubled.

SYLVIA: Less so now then before we met Mr. Barrie.

EMMA: I worry for him.

SYLVIA: Why don't you save your energy worrying about other things, Mother? Like your daughter-in-law as she prepares to birth her first child?

EMMA: I suppose I could drop in on my way home to check on her.

SYLVIA: Why don't you go now? The boys and I will be home shortly.

EMMA: Very well dear.

EMMA kisses SYLVIA on both cheeks, then exits.

SYLVIA shakes her head, glances at PETER, then sits on her blanket, STAGE LEFT, NICHOLAS on her lap.
BARRIE enters with PORTHOS. He notices PETER, then bends to PORTHOS and removes his lead.

BARRIE: Go and see Sylvia, Porthos. Good lad.

PORTHOS bounds off to see SYLVIA.

SYLVIA: Hello boy!

PORTHOS lies beside SYLVIA. BARRIE turns to PETER, walking over and sitting beside him on the bench. PETER doesn't look up.

BARRIE: On these magic shores children at play are forever beaching their coracles. We too have been there; we can still hear the sound of the surf, though we shall land no more.

PETER: Sorry?

BARRIE: It's from my play. What do you think?

PETER: It's out of context.

BARRIE: What do you think?

PETER: (**looking at Barrie, then sighing**) I suppose it sounds sad.

BARRIE: Sad? Why is that?

PETER: 'We shall land no more' sounds very final.

BARRIE: What do you think it means?

PETER: (**shrugs**) The loss of faith.

BARRIE: Faith in what?

PETER shrugs again.

PETER: Why are you asking me?

BARRIE: I think you've lost your faith, Peter.

PETER: Faith in what?

BARRIE: Anything. Everything. Youth. Joy. Love.

PETER: What do you know?

BARRIE: Not me, Peter, your uncle.

PETER: What has he said to you?

BARRIE: He is worried you have lost your spirit since your father died.

PETER turns his back on BARRIE. BARRIE pauses.

BARRIE: I lost someone when I was your age.

PETER doesn't respond.

BARRIE: Someone close to me, who taught me how to believe in magic.

PETER still doesn't respond.

BARRIE: I loved my brother David. He was the golden child of the family. My mother would promise him the world. When he died, I would do anything to help my mother. She lost faith. I even dressed in his clothes once. It was the first time my mother looked at me properly.

PETER inclines his head, listening.

BARRIE: Do you think your mother has lost her faith?

PETER: She loved my father.

BARRIE: I don't doubt she did. But Peter, there are other ways to help your mother without needing to replace your father.

PETER: Like how?

BARRIE: Believe. Stop trying to grow up so fast – it will happen in its own time. Enjoy your youth. Seeing you smile will help your mother more than all the grown up deeds in the world.

PETER doesn't answer, but he sees truth in BARRIES words.

BARRIE: I brought you something.

PETER inclines his head but does not turn.

BARRIE: Do you know why swallows build nests in the eaves of houses? It's to listen to stories. The best way to believe in magic is to create it yourself.

BARRIE pulls a new notebook from inside his jacket. He holds it out to PETER.

BARRIE: Write your own story, Peter.

PETER doesn't take the book.

BARRIE: Have faith. The moment you doubt whether you can fly, you cease forever to be able to do it.

PAUSE. PETER takes the book.

BARRIE: I think if you tried to remember what it means to be a child again, Peter, you would surprise yourself.

BARRIE gets to his feet and turns to walk to SYLVIA. However, he is disrupted by GEORGE running down the aisle. JACK and MICHAEL follow. They wear bandannas like pirates.

GEORGE: (**pointing at BARRIE and shouting**) Scurvy knave ahoy! Mr. Smee! Take him prisoner!

JACK: Aye-aye Captain!

JACK and MICHAEL run down the aisle and up the steps to BARRIE. GEORGE runs after them.

BARRIE removes his hat and wields his cane like a sword.

BARRIE: Arrr! Who ye calling a scurvy knave, I am nought but the perilous Captain Calypso of the good ship Mutiny! Ye shall bow to me or suffer the consequences and walk ye plank!

JACK, MICHAEL and GEORGE quickly drop to their knees.

JACK: Forgive us, great Captain, for we did not recognise you in your disguise!

BARRIE: Ye be Mr. Smee, aye?

JACK: Aye sir! Of the Jolly Roger!

BARRIE: Jolly Roger, ay, I have not heard of that ship! Who be your Captain!

GEORGE: That would be me, Sir!

BARRIE: That's Captain Sir to you! Stand, boy, and look me in the eye!

GEORGE stands and faces BARRIE. BARRIE surveys him.

BARRIE: How did a keel-rat like you become Captain! Mutiny, I wager!

GEORGE: Aye sir! I am the notorious Captain Anchor of the Jolly Roger and I will send you to the depths of the ocean!

BARRIE: Not Davy Jones Locker! I'm quaking in my boots!

GEORGE: En garde, ye old codfish!

BARRIE: Old! Who ye calling old!

JACK and MICHAEL: (**chanting**) Codfish, codfish, you are a codfish!

GEORGE and BARRIE engage in battle, stick against cane. BARRIE is disarmed and his sword sent flying backwards.

GEORGE: Any last words?!

BARRIE: You just wait until my first mate gets his sword in ye!

BARRIE looks over at PETER. PETER looks back, frowning. He then clicks on and falters. He grins suddenly, and hurries over, snatching up BARRIE'S cane. HE knocks GEORGE'S stick away.

PETER: Hands off my Captain, you bilge-rat! Any last words before I send you and your entire crew to the depths of Davey Jones Locker?!

GEORGE: You wouldn't do that to your brother would you!

PETER: Brother?! My mother sold me to pirates when I was but a wee lad! I have no brother!

GEORGE: Proud and insolent youth, prepare to meet thy doom!

PETER: Dark and sinister man! Have at thee!

PETER lunges at GEORGE, knocking him down. He then swipes and 'cuts off his right hand'. PETER swiftly stoops and pretends to throw the hand over board.

GEORGE: My hand! You picaroon!

PETER: Try fighting me now, codfish! Your hand is but a snack for the crocodiles!

PETER crows happily, then proceeds to wrestle his brothers. BARRIE gets to his feet and crosses to SYLVIA.

SYLVIA: How on earth did you do it?

BARRIE: Do what?

SYLVIA: Get him to play?

BARRIE: I restored his faith, just a little.

SYLVIA: The cleverness of you.

BARRIE: All this has happened before, and it will happen again.

**LIGHTS fade.
ACTORS exit.**

SCENE 10: THEATRE

**CURTAINS OPEN
LIGHTS RISE.**

BARRIE stands centre-stage, talking to CHARLES FROHMAN who stands beside him, arms folded.

BARRIE: And then the pirates attack, springing from nowhere, swords glinting!

CHARLES: Whoa, James, stop! Pirates? So far I have put up with you rabbiting on about fairies and a dog for a nursemaid – which is absurd by the way – but this is getting to be too much. Next you'll be wanting them to fly across the stage.

BARRIE stops and looks at CHARLES. CHARLES shakes his head.

CHARLES: No, James, no! It can't be done.

BARRIE: Believe, Charles. All we need is some ropes and harnesses and the rigging can be adjusted.

CHARLES: Do you know how crazy you sound right now? Shall I call bedlam?

BARRIE: Don't be silly, just hear me out.

CHARLES: You are talking about flying actors across the stage, suspended. Not just flying actors, but a boy who refuses to grow up. Absolutely ludicrous.

BARRIE: Think of the audience, Charles. It will be so spectacular that your sales will go through the roof!

CHARLES: Just like your mind. Up there, in the clouds... cuckoo.

BARRIE: You gave me one last chance, Charles, and this will work.

CHARLES raises an eyebrow and sighs.

CHARLES: Just don't add in anything else ridiculous, like a real pirate ship.

BARRIE avoids CHARLES gaze.

CHARLES: You've written in a full sized pirate ship, haven't you.

BARRIE: Not full sized.

CHARLES: Oh, not full sized, that's alright then!

CHARLES sighs.

CHARLES: I want a copy of this insane play of yours on my desk by Monday, understood? The play will premiere the day after boxing day.

BARRIE: Charles! You star!

CHARLES: Don't get too excited, it could all be for nought.

BARRIE: You need to have faith, Charles!

CHARLES: The only thing I *need* right now... is an enormous glass of gin.

**CHARLES exits STAGE RIGHT.
BARRIE turns to the audience and looks around.**

BARRIE: The boy who wouldn't grow up. It will be the biggest thing ever to grace the stage – I can feel it!

BARRIE as good as skips OFFSTAGE right.

The two fairies enter and dance around the stage as the curtains slowly close.

INTERVAL

SCENE 11: BARRIE MANOR

CURTAINS OPEN.

LIGHTS RISE.

BARRIE sits on the sofa, a letter in his hand. There are tears in his eyes as he reads.

BARRIE: (**reading**) "And so my dear, it is with great regret that I humbly request an enullment of this – what we have called – marriage. Though I loved you once, I have found it increasingly difficult to draw upon those feelings in recent months. You are a good man, James, with a big heart – and I can't help feeling you would be happier without me, free to live life the way you want. I regret what this may do to your social stature, but if your new play is to be as grand as you say then I can only hope that it will out-way the outcome of this separation. And so I leave you with a heavy heart, and a gentle goodbye, Mary Ansell."

BARRIE crumples the letter and holds it to his face, sobbing into it. He looks at the notebook in his other hand.

BARRIE: (**through tears**) What have you done to me? To my marriage? I never wanted this.

BARRIE drops his notebook and buries his head in his hands, clutching the letter.

PAUSE.

PETER PAN appears at the open window and quietly slips through it. HE creeps towards BARRIE, who doesn't notice, and picks up the notebook. He then sits cross-legged on the stage, flipping through the notebook. BARRIE looks up and starts, staring at PETER PAN. PETER PAN continues to flick through pages.

BARRIE: Who are you?

PETER PAN: I'm youth, I'm joy, I'm the little bird who has broken out of the egg!

BARRIE: Pan?

PETER PAN: The very same!

BARRIE: Where do you live?

PETER PAN: Second to the right and straight on til morning!

BARRIE: What a funny address!

PETER PAN: No it isn't!

BARRIE: I mean, is that what they put on the letters?

PETER PAN: Don't get letters.

BARRIE: But your Mother gets letters?

PETER PAN: Don't have a mother!

BARRIE: Oh, you poor thing!

PETER PAN: I'm alright. I live with boys – the lost boys!

BARRIE: And who are they?

PETER PAN: Children who fall out of their prams when nursemaids aren't looking. If they are not claimed in seven days, they are sent to the Never Never Land.

BARRIE: And there are no girls?

PETER PAN: Girls are far too clever to fall out of their prams.

BARRIE: Why are you here, Peter? Have you come to take me with you?

PETER PAN: You don't need to fly to Never Never Land, James. You're already there.

BARRIE: Then why are you here?

PETER PAN: Do you know why birds can fly and men cannot?

BARRIE: Why?

PETER PAN: Because birds have faith, for to have faith...

BARRIE: Is to have wings.

PETER PAN: Faith comes from happiness. It is not doing what you like, but in liking what you do that is the secret of happiness. Those who bring sunshine to the lives of others cannot keep it from themselves. You need to learn to fly again.

BARRIE: But I cannot fly.

PETER PAN: And why is that?

BARRIE: Because I am grown up. When people grow up, they forget the way.

PETER PAN: Why do they forget the way?

BARRIE: Because they are no longer innocent and heartless. It is only the innocent and heartless who can fly.

PETER PAN springs to the window.

PETER PAN: I can teach you! I'll teach you how to fly on the winds back, and then away we go! I'll teach you how to say funny things to the stars. Would you like an adventure now? Or shall we have our tea first?

PETER PAN fades through the window.
BARRIE watches him leave in awe.

BARRIE: Peter Pan...

LIGHTS FADE.
BARRIE exits.

SCENE 12: PARK

LIGHTS RISE.

GEORGE, JACK, MICHAEL and PETER hurry through the curtains, laughing and playing. They run around the front of the stage.

SYLVIA enters after them, pushing a pram and leaning on it heavily, struggling to stand. She walks towards the bench. She stops to cough into a handkerchief and flops onto the bench weakly.

JACK: (calling over) Mother? Did Uncle Jim say he was coming today?

SYLVIA: Yes darling.

MICHAEL: We haven't seen him in an enormous long time!

JACK: I want to show him my new ninja moves.

JACK karate chops PETER on the shoulder. PETER karate chops him back.

PETER: Hey, Jack! Do you want to be a ninja in my play?

JACK: Can I be the best ninja there ever was?

PETER: Of course!

GEORGE: Peter, can I be a pirate?! The most notorious cut throat ever to walk to earth!

BARRIE enters through the curtains, PORTHOS in hand.

MICHAEL: Like that one Uncle Gerald is playing in Jim's play?

GEORGE: Even more so!

BARRIE: Even more blood thirsty than Captain Hook! I dare say there isn't one!

GEORGE, JACK, PETER, MICHAEL: Uncle Jim!

JACK: Uncle Jim, I must show you my new moves!

PETER: I've written more pages too!

BARRIE: How marvellous! Might I say good morning to your Mother, and then my attention will be all yours?!

GEORGE: Aye!

JACK: Come on boys, let's go and come up with a game to play!

MICHAEL: Come on Porthos! You can be my great bear!

PORTHOS barks and follows MICHAEL. The BOYS and PORTHOS sit in a circle on the other side of the stage, deep in discussion.

BARRIE crosses to SYLVIA and makes a face at NICHOLAS in the pram.

BARRIE: Good morning, squire.

BARRIE kisses SYLVIA'S hand and sits beside her.

BARRIE: How are you this morning, Sylvia?

SYLVIA: I can't complain.

BARRIE frowns at her pale face, but shrugs. SYLVIA glances around.

SYLVIA: I thought Mary was going to join you today?

BARRIE carefully lays down his cane and removes his hat, disheartened.

BARRIE: Mary has moved out.

SYLVIA: Oh James, I am sorry.

BARRIE: She said she could no longer love a man who loved his work more than her. If I'm honest I knew it was coming.

SYLVIA: A week before the play opens as well.

BARRIE: She thought I would be too distracted to miss her.

BARRIE sighs.

BARRIE: Say, do your boys want to come and see the theatre? I can give them a behind the scenes tour of the play, show them how it all works.

SYLVIA: Oh James, I'm sure they'd love to!

BARRIE: Excuse me.

BARRIE picks up his cane and hat, stands and crosses to the boys.

BARRIE: Boys, I've got to head off now, but how would you like to come and sit in on a rehearsal?

GEORGE: Are you kidding?

JACK: That would be fantastic!

BARRIE: Good, get your things, I'll walk you there.

BARRIE leads the way back towards SYLVIA, the BOYS and PORTHOS behind him.

MICHAEL: Mother! Uncle Jim is going to take us to see his theatre!

PETER: Will you come, Mother?

SYLVIA: Actually, I was thinking of taking Nicholas home. I'm feeling a little under the weather. Uncle Gerry will be there.

PETER: Mother, are you alright?

SYLVIA: Just a little tired Peter darling. Nothing to worry about. You go on with Uncle Jim.

BARRIE frowns.

BARRIE: I'll have Gerald drop them home after rehearsal.

SYLVIA nods.

SYLVIA: Fantastic.

BARRIE begins to usher the boys away.

SYLVIA: James...

BARRIE: Aye?

SYLVIA: Remember to think happy thoughts.

BARRIE smiles and tips his hat to her, then hurries after the boys as they exit through the curtain.

SYLVIA pushes NICHOLAS after them and exits.

SCENE 13: THEATRE

CURTAINS OPEN.

The stage is set for PETER PAN NURSERY. Stagehands (dressed in Edwardian dress) and actors mill around the stage.

CHARLES FROHMAN enters STAGE LEFT, a pipe in his mouth, arms folded. He crosses to the bed and sits on it, looking around.

CHARLES: (admiring) What a mad man.

BARRIE enters STAGE RIGHT with GEORGE, JACK, PETER, MICHAEL and PORTHOS.

CHARLES: Ah, James.

CHARLES gets to his feet and walks over.

CHARLES: Are all of these yours, James?

BARRIE: No Charles, these are the Llewellyn-Davies boys I have told you about.

CHARLES: Ah, yes, your muses.

MICHAEL: (whispering to JACK) What's a moose?

BARRIE: I thought I'd give them a tour of the theatre and let them watch a bit of rehearsal. Their uncle is the Captain.

CHARLES: Yes yes, whatever. Just make sure they stay out of trouble.

BARRIE: Boys, why don't you sit there in the front row.

BARRIE points to the front of the stage. The BOYS and PORTHOS sit along the edge, their backs to the audience.

GEORGE: Isn't this exciting!

CHARLES: Can we go from scene two please!

STAGEHAND: Scene two!

The STAGEHANDS exit. CHARLES and BARRIE stand to the side of the stage, providing a full view of the scene.

HILDA, GEORGE H and WINIFRED enter STAGE RIGHT in Edwardian dress, with scripts in their hands.
They climb into beds and roll over to pretend to sleep.

PAUSE.

NINA appears at the window. Quietly she opens it and slips inside.

NINA: (whispering) Shadow? Oh, shadow?

MICHAEL: That's Peter Pan!

NINA searches the room, looking under beds and in boxes.
She sits on the floor, legs crossed with her hands over her face.

NINA: I'll never find it!

HILDA sits up in her bed.

HILDA: Boy, why are you crying?

NINA stands, her arms folded.

NINA: I wasn't crying!

The BOYS giggle.

NINA: I was trying to find my shadow.

HILDA: Your shadow?

NINA: Yes... I lost it here some nights ago.

HILDA: I know exactly where!

NINA: You do! Give it to me!

HILDA: You must say 'please'.

NINA: Please, please, oh please, I feel quite lost without it.

HILDA climbs out of bed and crosses to a trunk. She pulls out a shadow and kneels beside NINA.

HILDA: My dog, Nana, caught hold of it. I knew you were real but my Mother and Father... well... they didn't believe.

HILDA proceeds to start stitching the shadow on.

NINA: What is your name?

HILDA: Wendy Moira Angela Darling. What's yours?

NINA: Peter Pan.

HILDA: Is that all?

NINA: **(sulkily)** Yes.

HILDA: Where do you live?

NINA: Second to the right and straight on until morning.

HILDA: What a funny address.

NINA: No it isn't.

HILDA: What I mean is, is that what they put on the letters?

NINA: Don't get letters.

HILDA: But your Mother gets letters?

NINA: Don't have a mother.

HILDA: Oh you poor thing! No wonder you were crying!

NINA: I wasn't crying about Mothers.

HILDA sits back from sewing.

HILDA: There, good as new.

NINA stands with hands on hips.

NINA: Oh Wendy! Look ! The cleverness of me!

NINA crows excitedly.

HILDA: Of course, I did nothing.

NINA: You did a little.

HILDA: A little?!

HILDA climbs into bed with her covers over her head.

NINA: Oh Wendy, don't withdraw. I can't help crowing when I'm pleased with myself.

NINA crosses to the bed and sits cross legged on it.

NINA: Wendy? One girl is worth more than twenty boys.

HILDA pulls the cover down.

HILDA: Do you really think so?

NINA nods.

HILDA: I think its perfectly lovely the way you talk about girls. I think I should like to give you a kiss.

NINA: A kiss? What's a kiss?

HILDA: Don't you know?

NINA: I shall know when you give me one.

NINA closes her eyes, her hand outstretched. HILDA crosses to the chest and pulls out a thimble, placing it in NINA'S palm.

CHARLES: (**hushed**) How absurd.

NINA and HILDA stop acting and look over at CHARLES. WINIFRED and GEORGE H sit up and look over too.

BARRIE: Oh Charles, can't you get in touch with your youth for a short while?

CHARLES: A thimble?

BARRIE: It's a very sweet gesture. You see, both Peter and Wendy are young. What does a kiss mean to children?

MICHAEL: Our Mother kisses us goodnight before she turns the nightlight on. It means she is protecting us.

BARRIE: You see Charles?

CHARLES: What did you boys think of the play?

The BOYS stand, except PETER.

GEORGE: I think it was marvellous!

MICHAEL: Yes, Uncle Jim, I think it was the bestest there ever was!

JACK: Are they to fly Uncle Jim?

BARRIE: Oh yes, Jack, they are to fly.

The BOYS gasp excitedly.

BARRIE: In fact, why don't you boys go backstage with the actors. I'm sure they would love to show you how it all works.

NINA and HILDA hold their hands out to the boys. GEORGE, MICHAEL and JACK hurry excitedly over.

NINA, HILDA, GEORGE, MICHAEL, JACK, CHARLES, GEORGE H and WINIFRED exit STAGE RIGHT.

PETER stays sat, staring at the set.

BARRIE: Are you alright Peter?

PETER turns so he is facing out to the audience. He swings his legs over the edge of the stage. BARRIE sits beside him, leaning on his cane.

PETER: What happens next?

BARRIE: In the play? (**Peter nods**) Peter Pan shows the Darling children how to fly.

PETER: Then what?

BARRIE: Off they go to Never Neverland for marvellous adventures.

PETER: Must they?

BARRIE: Do you not want them to, laddie?

PETER doesn't answer.

BARRIE: What's on your mind, Peter?

PETER pauses, playing with his hands. He takes a while to respond.

PETER: It's Mother.

BARRIE: What about her?

PETER: She's sick. She denies it – but I can tell. It's the same as what happened with Father.

BARRIE: I'm sure she'll be fine Peter.

PETER stands, suddenly angry.

PETER: Grown ups always say that! Grown ups always lie.

BARRIE: Peter, I'm not lying to you.

PETER: You are! I'm sick of grown ups! I wish I could fly away to Never Neverland and never have to worry about grown up things again.

PETER runs off towards his siblings. BARRIE stands and watches him go, frowning. He exits sadly.

SCENE 14: PARK

PORTHOS bounds through the curtain barking. He sniffs around for a moment. BARRIE enters shortly afterwards. He carries a ball.

BARRIE: You daft dog, Porthos, I still have the ball in my hand!

PORTHOS bounds around his feet.

BARRIE: It's opening night tomorrow, laddie. Are we ready?

PORTHOS barks.

BARRIE: Aye, I thought you'd say that.

BARRIE bends to stroke PORTHOS.

BARRIE: *as PORTHOS* Don't worry, Mr. Barrie, those who bring sunshine to the lives of others cannot keep it from themselves.

BARRIE stands and throws the ball for PORTHOS. PORTHOS bounds after it. BARRIE watches him.
GEORGE enters through the curtain and approaches BARRIE.

GEORGE: Uncle Jim?

BARRIE: Hello George! How are you? Are you alone?

GEORGE: (**nods**) My brothers stayed home today with Grandmother.

BARRIE: Are they alright?

GEORGE: They're alright, yes.

BARRIE: And your mother?

GEORGE: (**hesitantly**) She's sick. The doctor said it would be unwise for her to leave the house for a few days.... which means...

Both BARRIE and GEORGE know the true nature of the illness – and what is likely to happen.

BARRIE: She can't make the play tomorrow night.

The Lost Boy | 58

GEORGE: She sends her apologies.

BARRIE: Don't be daft, laddie, I understand.

GEORGE: I'll be bringing the boys though... Uncle Gerry has given us some of his seats.

BARRIE: Good. (**pause**) I'll come round to see her in a day or two. Give her my best, wont you?

GEORGE: Of course, Uncle Jim.

BARRIE: Are you and the boys alright with your Grandmother?

GEORGE: Yes.

BARRIE: Your Grandmother means well.

GEORGE: I know. (**taking his hat off**) See you tomorrow night, Uncle Jim.

GEORGE replaces his hat and exits.

BARRIE: See you tomorrow night, laddie.

PORTHOS brings the ball back.

BARRIE: I suppose it's like the ticking crocodile, isn't it? Time is chasing after all of us.

PORTHOS barks knowingly. BARRIE leads him offstage through the curtain.

SCENE 15: THEATRE - OPENING NIGHT

EMMA and PETER enter from the rear of the auditorium. EMMA holds PETER's hand.

PETER: I can't believe it's opening night already! Won't it be fantastic Grandmother!

EMMA: I believe it will, Peter.

PETER: I like Mr. Barrie. He's really helped Mother.

EMMA: (**sadly**) I see that now.

PETER: I know you don't like him, Grandmother...

EMMA: Now now. I do like Mr. Barrie. He has done wonders for you, and for your Mother. I am eternally grateful to him for that.

PETER: Uncle Gerry likes him too.

EMMA: Your Uncle Gerry is too kind for his own good.

PETER: He's excited about starring in the play.

EMMA: As a Pirate? (**sarcastically**) Yes – really the highlight of his career. People will be talking about him for years. No, Peter, this play will be wonderful for now but it will soon be forgotten.

PETER: Mother believes in it.

EMMA: If only Sylvia could be here.

PETER: (**bravely**) She'll be alright after she's had a rest, grandmother. George and Jack will take good care of her.

EMMA: You have done well taking the role of your Father, Peter.

PETER: Someone had to be the grown up.

EMMA: Come. We should take our seat.

EMMA and PETER take their reserved seats in the front row.

CHARLES enters through the curtain in OPENING NIGHT attire. He takes in the audience and grins.

CHARLES: Nothing I like better than opening night.

CHARLES descends the steps and approaches the audience. He interacts with them, nodding and shaking hands.

CHARLES:　　Good evening
　　　　　　　Isn't this exciting
　　　　　　　He's a madman, an absolute madman
　　　　　　　Have you attended a Barrie play before?

HOUSE LIGHTS FLICKER.

CHARLES: Ah! It's almost time!

CHARLES returns to STAGE LEFT and checks his pocket-watch.

BARRIE enters, waving jovially at PETER, before joining CHARLES.

CHARLES: Don't let me down, James.

BARRIE: Have you seen this auditorium, Charles? Scarcely an empty seat anywhere. This will be a show to be remembered for generations to come, you just watch.

CHARLES: (**unconvinced**) Mmm.

BARRIE: Just watch.

CURTAINS OPEN on the PETER PAN BEDROOM SET.

PAUSE.

WINIFRED, playing Michael Darling, enters STAGE RIGHT, carrying a teddy bear. NANA enters after her.

She stands CENTRESTAGE and stamps her foot.

WINIFRED: I won't go to bed! I won't! I won't!

NANA barks. WINIFRED squeaks. The BOYS giggle. BARRIE points at MICHAEL with a twinkling smile.

WINIFRED: But it's not even six o clock yet! Two minutes more!

NANA barks again.

WINIFRED: One minute more?!

**NANA barks again. WINIFRED jumps into bed.
HILDA enters as Wendy Darling, carrying a book.**

HILDA: John dear, hurry along with your things.

GEORGE H enters as John Darling, carrying a pirate sword and wearing a pirate hat.

GEORGE H: Yes Wendy.

HILDA: Michael, stop giving Nana cheek.

HILDA tucks WINIFRED up.

HILDA: Would you like a story before lights out?

WINIFRED: Oh, yes please Wendy!

GEORGE H climbs into bed.

GEORGE H: Will there be pirates?!

WINIFRED: And Indians!

GEORGE H: And mermaids!

WINIFRED: And Peter Pan?!

HILDA: I dare say so. Now... let's see... All children except one grow up. They may not want to, but eventually they must...

**LIGHTS FADE. ACTORS 'sleep'.
LIGHTS RISE. NINA as Peter Pan stands in the doorway, hands outstretched. It is later in the play.**

HILDA kneels in front of the window. GEORGE H and WINIFRED stand by her.

NINA: Come away with me where you'll never have to worry about grown up things again.

HILDA: Never is an awfully long time, Peter.

NINA: I'll teach you to ride on the wind's back, and away we go!

HILDA takes NINA'S hand.

LIGHTS FADE. HILDA lies in the middle of the stage, as though unconscious. ACTORS playing SLIGHTLY, TOOTLES and CURLY enter and stand with their backs to HILDA. NINA stands in stance.

LIGHTS RISE.

NINA: Good news, boys! I have brought a Mother for you all at last! Have you not seen her? She flew this way.

NINA looks. The LOST BOYS look to one another.

SLIGHTLY: Ah, woeful day.

NINA: Why is that?

TOOTLES: Back boys, I will let Peter see.

NINA: Let Peter see what?

THE LOST BOYS look to one another and then step to one side.

CURLY: She is dead.

NINA: (**kneeling beside HILDA**) Perhaps she is frightened at being dead? Whos arrow?!

TOOTLES: Twas mine, Peter. (**he kneels**) Strike Peter, strike true!

HILDA stirs as NINA raises her knife.

NINA: The Wendy lady! She lives!

LIGHTS FADE. NINA kneels DOWNSTAGE RIGHT. GERALD as Captain Hook enters DOWNSTAGE RIGHT, his back to NINA.

LIGHTS RISE ON DOWNSTAGE RIGHT.

GERALD: Who are you, stranger! Speak!

NINA: (**in a deep voice**) I am James Hook! Captain of the Jolly Roger!

GERALD: You are not!

NINA: Brimestone and gall! Say that again and I will cast anchor in you!

GERALD: If you are Hook, then tell me, who am I?!

NINA: A codfish!

The BOYS laugh.

GERALD: A codfish! Hook! Have you another voice?!

NINA: I have!

GERALD: And another name?!

NINA: Aye!

GERALD: Vegetable!?

NINA: No!

GERALD: Mineral!

NINA: No!

GERALD: Animal!

NINA: Yes!

GERALD: Man?!

NINA: No!

GERALD: Boy?!

NINA: Yes!

GERALD: Ordinary boy?!

NINA: No!

GERALD: Wonderful boy?!

NINA: Yes! Do you give up?!

GERALD pulls his revolver out of his coat. NINA stands.

NINA: I ... am...!

GERALD points the gun at NINA.

GERALD: History!

GERALD pulls the trigger. As he does, the LIGHT FADES. LIGHT RISES on NINA and HILDA knelt in the spotlight.

HILDA: Shall we swim or fly, Peter?

NINA: Do you think you could swim or fly as far as the island, Wendy, without my help?

HILDA: I don't think so. Why can you not?

NINA: I can't help you, Wendy. Hook wounded me. I can neither fly nor swim.

HILDA: Do you mean we shall both be drowned?

NINA: Look how the water is rising!

NINA and HILDA cover their eyes. NINA peeks through hers and looks up.

NINA: Michael's kite! It lifted Michael off the ground... why should it not carry you?!

HILDA: Both of us!?

NINA: It won't carry two. Michael and Curly tried.

HILDA: Let us draw lots.

NINA: And you a lady? Never!

NINA 'ties' HILDA with the kite string.

NINA: Goodbye Wendy!

HILDA is pulled out of the light.

NINA: To die would be an awfully big adventure.

LIGHTS FADE. Sound of a bell jingling faintly.

LIGHTS RISE.

NINA kneels on the ground again, holding 'Tinkerbell' in her hands.

NINA: Poisoned? But who could have poisoned it? (**BELL**) Hook?! The codfish! Oh Tink, you drank it to save me. (**BELL**) Your light! It is going out! Oh Tink, please don't die. I need you!

USHER approaches BARRIE with a letter.

USHER: Sir... this has just come for you.

BARRIE takes the letter and opens it.

BARRIE: (reading aloud) My dear James. It saddens me that this letter must reach you during your opening night.

BARRIE and SYLVIA (offstage): I do believe...

SYLVIA: (offstage) however that I may not get chance again to see you. The doctor has just been, you see, and things do not look good. It is my solemn wish to bid you goodbye, and I hope you will do all in your power to take care of my dear sons.

BARRIE closes the paper and turns to CHARLES.

BARRIE: I'm sorry Charles, I must be somewhere. I will be back.

**BARRIE hastily exits into the darkness.
FOCUS back on NINA.**

NINA: **(BELL – NINA looks to the audience)** Do you believe in fairies?! If you believe... clap your hands!

The BOYS stand and clap their hands excitedly. The audience are encouraged to join in.

NINA: Tinkerbell! You're alive! And now! To rescue Wendy!!

LIGHTS FADE. NINA exits. BOYS sit.

LIGHTS RISE on STAGE LEFT.

**SYLVIA sits in the bed, looking ill, a book on her knee.
BARRIE hurries in.**

SYLVIA: James?!

BARRIE sits on the edge of her bed.

SYLVIA: You should be at the play!

BARRIE: The play will go ahead without me. I needed to see you.

SYLVIA: You got my letter?

BARRIE: Yes. I needed to tell you something. (**he takes her hand**) This saying goodbye nonsense. Never say goodbye, because goodbye means going away and going away means forgetting.

SYLVIA: Then I shall say farewell instead. (**she coughs whole-bodiedly**) Were the audience enjoying themselves?

BARRIE: They seemed to be.

SYLVIA: (**she coughs again**) I wish I could see it.

BARRIE: There are other nights. You could always make one of those.

SYLVIA: (**shakes her head**) I mean Neverland, James. Will you take me there?

BARRIE: (**nods slowly**) Shut your eyes.

SYLVIA shuts her eyes. BARRIE does too.

The Lost Boy | 67

BARRIE: Do you see a shapeless pool of colours suspended in the darkness?

SYLVIA: Yes.

BARRIE: Squeeze your eyes tighter and the pool begins to take shape. The colours become so vivid that with another squeeze they must go on fire.

SYLVIA: I see it! I'm there, James!

BARRIE: Listen to the mermaids as they sing.

MERMAIDS enter and sit on the edge of the stage, silently beckoning.

BARRIE: They are calling for you to join them.

SYLVIA: How lovely.

PIRATES enter, creeping.

BARRIE: And the Pirates, watch they don't catch you.

INDIANS enter, creeping.

BARRIE: Listen as the Indians chant.

FAIRIES enter, dancing.

BARRIE: The fairies are here too, asking you to come and dance with them.

SYLVIA: I cannot join them without Peter Pan.

BARRIE: We will watch from here then, for just a moment.

BARRIE and SYLVIA remain where they are for a moment, eyes open and watching the characters. They do not react when HILDA enters and stands at the head of the bed as WENDY, or when the window opens and NINA stands framed as PETER PAN.

SYLVIA: What if I must leave Neverland?

HILDA: What if I must grow up?

SYLVIA and HILDA: I shall never see you again.

NINA and BARRIE: You know that place between asleep and awake? That place where you still remember dreaming? That's where I will always love you. That's where I'll be waiting.

HILDA fades into the shadows. SYLVIA looks towards BARRIE, then at NINA in the window.

SYLVIA: Peter Pan is here, James. He is here to take me to Never Neverland with him.

BARRIE kisses SYLVIA'S hand and stands up.

BARRIE: Second to the right and straight on until morning.

NINA hops through the window and up to the bed, taking SYLVIA'S hand. NINA leads her out of bed and to the window.

NINA: So come with me where dreams are born and time is never planned. Just think of happy things and your heart will fly on wings, forever, in Never-Never-Land.

NINA leads SYLVIA through the window and out of sight. BARRIE turns to the window and removes his hat, walking to it and looking out.

BARRIE: The window will always be open for you.

LIGHTS FADE.

The BOYS stand and walk to the STAGE RIGHT steps, lining up along them.

EMMA DU MAURIER enters STAGE LEFT and stands with CHARLES.

LIGHTS RISE for CURTAIN CALL.

CURTAIN CALL.
THE END.

The original 2015 cast + director

The Llewelyn-Davies boys play pirates in the park

Barrie and the boys play Indians in the park

Opening night of 'Peter Pan'.

Gerald DuMurier was the original Captain Hook

Barrie says goodbye to Sylvia.

Our original cast

J.M. Barrie and the boys

Made in the USA
Coppell, TX
26 January 2023